First Day Love

Wardell Henderson

ISBN 978-1-0980-2602-8 (paperback)
ISBN 978-1-0980-2603-5 (digital)

Christian Faith Publishing, Inc.
832 Park Avenue
Meadville, PA 16335
www.christianfaithpublishing.com

Printed in the United States of America

I woke this morning with a prayer for all prayers. I asked the Lord to make this first day of school a very special one. I wanted nothing more than his blessings for my life, and school was not excluded since I would be spending most of my day there. On my knees and hands folded, I prayed that he would send love, patience, and friendship coupled with obedience today because the first day of school often determines what the remainder of the school will mimic.

As I was finishing my prayers, I remembered that my parents were struggling just to make ends meet on the farm and they also needed a blessing, so I asked God to watch over them and our farm today.

My name is Hoakey Lewis, and this will be my first day of school in the tenth grade.

Opening my window and sticking my head out, I realized that this was going to be a hot sticky morning. I turned to get ready for school. I selected jean shorts and a Black Crowes tee-shirt I got at a concert this summer, my Air Jordan sneakers which I got also this summer from the Big Q-Mart.

I went in to have breakfast as my mom and dad were patiently awaiting my arrival. It smelled good as I rounded the corner. Taking a seat, we held hands and blessed the food, our lives, and the people of our community.

"Are you all excited about high school?" my dad asked.

"Yes, sir, I can't wait to get started."

My mom smiled, then turned to remind me that I had to eat before the bus arrived. Afterward, I grabbed my book bag, walked to the door with them, and we hugged.

"Don't forget your father," my mother said.

I nodded and ran down the drive to the bus stop three houses over.

The school bus will be here shortly, and all the other guys and I will meet at the bus stop and talk about our summer vacation and, of course, girls. At the stop already are Gary, Sammy, Glen, Jake Jr., and a new kid. He tells us his name is Mickey and he moved here from Iowa. This is one of two stops in our town and it's directly in front of Glen's house. Some of the kids have to be driven here and dropped off because of where their homes are located off the road. They walk home after the school bus drops them off from school. Most of them enjoy walking and chatting about their day.

A few feet away, it looked to be about ten girls awaiting the bus also, and Sebrina Rae is one of them. She's really nice looking. I've wanted to ask her to the barn dance last year but keep getting butterflies. Our eyes meet and she smiles. The other guys see and begin to rag on me. You can hear the girls giggling afterward. I turned away and gathered myself. I rejoined the conversation with the guys, and soon after, I noticed a large truck coming down the road. We moved out of the road to allow it to get by without having to ride in the middle of the street. It rode by so fast that it blew the girls' skirts about. We laughed as they tried to hold their skirts down. The girls gave us the look of payback, so we stopped laughing.

Mickey begins telling us about himself, the city life, and with all the excitement he had. Boy, he had it made. The bus arrives before anyone else could talk of his or her summer adventures. We catch the bus because the school is in the city and we live in the farming area of town. We don't come to the city much because there is much work to be done after school and on weekends to keep the farms running. Of course, we do get to town every now and then.

As we board the bus, we let the girls board first so that we could see who is the prettiest or who had gotten fat over the summer. It gives us something to talk about with each other, and I guess they are talking about us also.

To our surprise, each girl is sitting alone. We stroll on the bus, having to secure a seat next to a girl as if it were designed seating. We look at each other's face not having to say a word; the message was clear. We've been set up. The bus stops at the next stop and three guys get on. Their mouths pop open as they notice the seating arrangements, and we all shake our heads at the same time. Fortunately, the bus only makes these two stops and we're off to school.

As it begins pulling away, a car horn blows and the car pulls in front of the bus and the driver stops. Out of the car pops a girl. She gets aboard, and immediately the door closes and off we go. Yes, she is a beautiful girl with baby brown hair and green eyes gets on the bus as the car pulls away.

So happened, all the guys notice and sit straight in their seats. She finds a seat directly across from me and then the thing you only see in the movies or on television happens. She introduces herself and instead of saying my name, I blurt out gibberish.

Sebrina Rae interrupts and says, "His name is Hoakey and he's shy. I'm Sebrina Rae, and you are?"

"My name is Nikole Parker, and we're from Abingdon, Maryland. My father got transferred here as the new bank president. He wanted to live away from the city so we live out here. We moved into the old Guillaume place."

"Wow," says Sebrina Rae, "that's great."

As I sat listening, I wondered what the guys were thinking now. They knew I liked Sebrina Rae, but the look on my face for Nikole wasn't fear; it was excitement.

I sat still with the goofy-looking smile and sweaty palms. I tried looking around, only to see a girl smiling at me and I lowered my head. Thoughts ran through my head like none I had ever experienced. I kept getting mixed up, trying to get it together. I decided to take a deep breath, and all of a sudden, I felt relaxed.

The bus pulled into the school, and what looked like hundreds of other kids stood outside talking. Some I knew from middle school.

As we got off the bus, Nikole said, "Hoakey, I hope you weren't embarrassed."

I smiled and said no. Sammy who was walking alongside of me then pushed me and said, "Got a new girlfriend, uh? What's Sebrina Rae going to say when the word gets out that you have a crush on the new girl?"

I was silent for a moment as Nikole watched, and then I said, "Big deal." Nikole just smiled.

While in my homeroom, I sat alone thinking of Nikole's green eyes and the way she looked at me. Boy, I must be looking awfully goofy and dazed about now. As my name was called, hearing it, I uttered as a response, "Here, Mrs. Nikole."

As laughter shattered the room, Mrs. Grable ask for quiet, then said, "Mr. Lewis, is there something you'd like to share with the class?"

I said, "No, there isn't. Is something wrong?"

She stated that I called her Mrs. Nikole.

At that very moment, I lowered my head, truly in embarrassment. What a way to start the morning. I know I asked God for a great first day however I think He is testing my faith.

After homeroom as I was heading to my first class, I noticed both Sammy and Jake Jr. talking with Sebrina Rae. I slowed down a bit to avoid any unwelcome words from Sebrina Rae. Even as I slowed my pace, they all turned toward me as if to say here he is now. I ventured over to see what was going on as if I didn't already know, only to get a frown from Sebrina Rae.

"Hey there Mr. Casanova, playboy, lover-boy," Sebrina Rae says.

I turn to look at the guys and see that they have grins on their faces.

Before I could say anything, a girl from my ninth grade class last year spoke to me. Her name was Regina. I hadn't seen her all summer. She asked how I'd been and we made brief small talk. She then asks which way I was going and could I walk with her to class.

Before I could answer, I felt the heat from those blue eyes of Sebrina Rae piercing my neck as Sammy and Jake Jr. stood grinning.

I replied yes and uttered a quick "see you guys later." As Regina and I walked to the next class which I found we had together, I got a pinch on my butt. Turning to look, I stared right into those green eyes of Nikole.

"Is this your girlfriend?" she asked.

I replied, "No, she is a friend. Nikole, this is Regina Underae."

They spoke and Nikole said that she hopes to see me at lunch so that she could ask me something. Regina smiled, and after Nikole walked off, said, "She likes you."

I said, "Yeah right."

Regina asked if Sammy had a girlfriend. I looked at her and said, "Sammy, my friend Sammy?"

"Yes, Sammy."

I said, "Nope, no one I know."

She appeared relieved. We went in to our math class and I told her that I'd put in a good word.

"No!" She said, "I can speak for myself and will when the time is right. You must promise me you won't say a word to him."

"I promise."

During class, my focus was interrupted every time I thought about Regina and Sammy. He was an odd character in his own way and never really considered having a girlfriend even though we spoke of girls. I found myself giggling and looked up and saw Regina giving me the eye. After class changed, we walked out together and she reminded me of my promise, then we parted. She also said that if I told anyone that she'd tell everyone that I slept with a stuffed baby lamb each night. I laughed and said that she could tell anyone she liked.

"Oh yeah," she says.

"Yeah! You see, I sleep with my lamb because I believe in the Lamb of God and my little lamb reminds me of Jesus. It keeps me close to God as I sleep. So if you like, you could tell everyone and I will tell them what I told you. Now, do you sleep with any dolls or bears?"

Her mouth opened but no words came out only the nodding.

"Are we good?" I asked.

"Yes," she said, "we're good."

My next class was English. I went directly there. Noticing all the other students were quiet, I looked up to see who the teacher was. He looked to be as big and strong as a bear. Muscles everywhere and had a look on his face that warned you not to try anything in his class. In fact, he was the only African American teacher in the entire school.

The bell rang; he closed the door and who opened it but Sebrina Rae. She had been running. She was out of breath and at the same time was handing the teacher a note. He said thanks and asked her to be seated. As she found a seat, he read the note, then placed it on his desk next to what appeared to be a desk clock.

Not noticing, the only remaining seat was across from me. Girls on both sides, that's just great. Sebrina Rae whispered that she didn't want to hear anything from me in a slightly angered voice and I obliged her.

Sebrina Rae did nothing but stare for the first few minutes of class. She then took a deep breath and said, "I heard that you and the new girl Nikole are dating? Boy, you move fast. What, I'm not pretty enough for you anymore? I swear, you think you know someone. You could have told me you weren't interested in me, don't you think? I would not have wasted my summer thinking about you as much as I did. I'm hurt, however I hope we can still be friends. Can we?"

My throat felt dry listening to her speak and all I could do was nod.

As I was about to answer, I noticed this big shadow between our desks.

"Go ahead, Mr. Lewis, it is Lewis, isn't it?"

"Well, sir, she asked me a question."

"I know and until you clear this up, I won't have any peace in my class."

"Yes, sir."

I looked over at Sebrina Rae and she had her head between her arms as if she were embarrassed. So I say, "Sebrina Rae, it wasn't like that. Nikole and I are friends as are we."

I looked up and all the class was giggling at us.

"All right," she said, "now leave me alone."

Mr. Ward said, "Thank you and the class thanks you too. There will be no talking in class unless you are asked or are answering a question. Is that understood?"

"Yes, sir," we all replied.

Sebrina Rae was steaming about now. She had been embarrassed on her first day in class.

During class, I could feel her eyes piercing my skin. You know that type of look you get when someone is planning a way to get you back for a prank or a joke. I wasn't prepared for Sebrina Rae at least not on the first day of school. I couldn't believe she thought about me over the summer. How was I supposed to know? I guess it doesn't matter now, does it?

Before class let out, she slipped me a note. She said that she was going to give it to me earlier. I didn't want to take it because I felt that she was wanted me to feel bad for what had happened. I slipped the note in my pocket and went to my next class which was study hall.

I had study hall during the next period with Gary, Glen, and Mickey. Mr. Queve was in charge of this study period. He was nice and asked that we do what we needed quietly so as not to disturb anyone studying. Study hall was a way of allowing us to relax between classes. I was glad I had it with the guys.

We finally got to talk about our summer vacation and of course girls. There was so much excitement that we had to cut it short. Not the subject of girls. Glen met a pretty redhead with freckles and all while visiting an aunt in Charlevoix, Michigan, for his summer vacation. He even got a real kiss and a picture together. Can you believe that? Lucky guy!

At that moment, I remembered the note and I slipped it out of my pocket. Reading it, it said, "I think you are cute, but please make up your mind quick. Hopefully, you will let me know at lunch." It was signed with a smiley face. I smiled.

Mickey, who came from a town with excitement had been kissed on many occasions and had been out to the movies a couple of times, alone with his girlfriend. I myself had only dreamed of Sebrina Rae and my holding her hand. The only kisses I got were from my mother.

Sebrina Rae always pretended to be better than us. She'd always walk with her head and nose in the air. It didn't bother me any, but I did notice. Now, Nikole was different. She was like an angel without wings. Even though she was pretty, she didn't put on like Sebrina Rae. I didn't think that I would ever feel this way. Guess you don't know until it happens to you. I think I'm going to ask her to our first school dance.

I can't keep the secret any longer and have to tell the guys. At that very moment, I had to ask the Lord for forgiveness in not keeping the news of Regina and Sammy quiet. I think that he understood and forgave me. So I let it out.

"Hey, guys, you know Regina Underae from ninth grade, well, she likes good ole Sammy."

In my mind, I asked the Lord and Regina to forgive me for telling the guys. I told her I wouldn't tell him. She's going to herself.

"Isn't that scary, Sammy with a girl. Please don't say anything to him. Let's wait to see what he does when she tells him."

The guys agreed. That was a big relief having shared that with someone. I think I was going to burst holding that in any longer.

Well, study hall is ending and another class is about to start. I yelled back that I'll catch you guys at lunch. Lunch was held at the same time for the entire school.

It was time for science class. After sitting down, I said a little prayer because I wasn't that good in science and everyone needs a little help. They said that Mr. Pede was a geek. With stripped pants, a plaid shirt buttoned to the top, colorful bowties, and thick glasses. It is said that he takes mice and lets them sit on his shoulders. I was also told that he gives an assignment on the very first day of class. I certainly wasn't prepared for that if that's his pattern.

I can't wait to get started in his class. He closes the door, calls roll, and immediately pairs us up. I was paired with none other than Sammy. I couldn't help but to giggle. Just thinking of he and Regina together was funny. I moved my things from my area to where our worktable was located and settled in.

Mr. Pede stated that he would bring around an animal to each table so that we could be familiar with them. We got the usual frog. I guess later in the year we'll cut him up or something.

As we sat watching Mr. Pede write on the blackboard, the frog jumped from one side of the desk to the other. Sammy was startled. I laughed and everyone turned toward me wondering what was going on, even the two girls that had the snake as their assignment looked on.

By then, I found myself telling Sammy what I had learned from a girl I met. I didn't tell him her name. He started blushing. I was surprised thinking that he may have blurted out something stupid. He said, "Really, I can't believe a girl was interested in me. When do you think I can meet her?"

I giggled and said, "Be patient, and it will happen when it happens."

I asked him not to mention it to others even the guys. In my mind, I asked the Lord to help me to keep my mouth closed because I made a promise that I didn't fully keep. The devil is always busy; however, the Lord curved my tongue before I said anything further. Mr. Pede stated that we would be having a crossword quiz and that we could complete it as a team and to place it on his desk on the way out of class. Surprisingly, Sammy was up to speed and we finished rather quickly. He stared me down in hopes that I would reveal who the girl was. I spoke of the possibility of going out for the football team since our season was different than other states. We only played the other schools within the three counties and the winner played in the state semi-finals. I said to the guys that if they wanted to play practice would be during PE and a selection would be made by this afternoon. That's because our school is small and that most guys wanted to play baseball instead of football. Our chances of making the team is very high since they weren't selective to the point of seeking top quality players.

"I'm in," he said, "and what position do you think you're going to play?"

"I wanted to be selected as a receiver," I said. He laughed. That seemed to distract him somewhat.

With all the excitement, the class bell rang, Sammy dropped our paper on Mr. Pede's desk and it was off to math class.

On the way, I stopped by my locker to drop off some unneeded books that I'll pick up on my way home. For some reason, I became nervous, and trying to open my locker was like having a splinter in my finger. It was tough and I finally got it opened and ran off to class.

In the classroom were pictures all over the walls of really old people, the majority men. On the ceiling were various sized and colored balls on clear string hanging at different levels. I thought, *Cool, this is gonna be a neat class.*

Our teacher whose nameplate sat on a big wooden frame was named Mrs. Lampo. She walked right in when the bell rang and introduced herself. She said, "I pray that everyone had a great summer." Then she asked us to introduce ourselves and tell a little about who we were. That was kind of embarrassing because we were all nervous and stuttering. When the last kid finished, we all clapped.

Ms. Lampo said that the seats we were now sitting would be the assigned seats and that we could change now if we wanted. As no one moved, she said fine. She began handing out our assignments for the quarter, and we began reading them to ourselves however without noticing, out loud. She asked was there a problem? Okay then, let's get started.

We began almost where we left off in the ninth grade as if we didn't even have a summer break. As Ms. Lampo asked questions, hands all over were raised. We either knew the answer or we figured it out on the blackboard. The class played a numeric association exercise. It was fun and everyone enjoyed it. Ms. Lampo said, "This is what class will be like each term if you like or our focus could come from the textbook. So what would you like?"

We all shouted out different responses having the same meaning.

She said, "Well, it's decided. Please pass all the assignment sheets forward so that I will collect them. We won't need them after all."

In my mind, I could hear myself say, "Thank you, Jesus." After which, she handed out an assignment sheet with games, fun problem solving, and other interesting math for each week.

We were having so much fun that the bell had already rang for class change.

I went again to my locker to put up my books and headed for lunch to meet the guys.

I was so excited about the math assignment that I was going over it in my head as I walked to the cafeteria. Until I actually heard the noise and smelled the food, I had no idea that I had arrived.

I saw the guys about halfway in the line. I got in about the tenth person back. The line moved quickly. As I was getting my milk, I saw both Sebrina Rae and Nikole. No, they weren't together but at the same time. I prayed that they wouldn't see me right away because I didn't want to be in the middle of two

girls. As I walked away from the serving line, I heard Nikole ask me to save her a seat. Not realizing it, I shook my head, saying, "Yeah, okay."

Sitting down near the end, Sammy asks, "Are you going to tell me or what? I just want to know who she is."

Then right across was Regina giving me that look. I turned to Sammy telling him that he'd find out soon enough and left it at that. I could see on his face that he wasn't too happy with that response. I started saying my grace before eating not realizing that Nikole had sat down.

"That's a nice prayer. Do you pray before each meal?"

"Yes, I give thanks to God because He takes care of us for all of our needs."

"Can you teach me?"

"Yes," I said. "No matter what you do in life, whether it's good or bad, pray for forgiveness and thanks. At home we give thanks before each meal, at bedtime, and in the morning before we do anything, pray for a blessed day, safety and love in all that we do and say to one another. I think that you should start praying daily. I know in my heart it will make your life more meaningful as you establish a personal relationship with God. That's really what it is about, having a relationship with him and He will provide all of your needs. Do you understand now why prayer is essential?"

Looking bewildered, she nodded. I thought she was crying because her eyes were teary.

"Are you all right, I mean is everything OK?"

"Yes, thank you," she says. "You are a special person and I am happy that we are friends."

Silence consumed the space we shared for nearly three minutes straight, then out of the blue, she asks, "Did you miss me?"

After, taking a deep breath, I said yes.

Taking a break from chewing, Nikole said that she wanted to know even though today is the first day of school do I have a girl friend? All I could do was think for that moment to say softly was "Thank you, Jesus." Then the word "no" sputtered from my lips.

"Well," she asked, "would you like to go steady?"

The food in my throat got stuck. I immediately took a swallow of milk. I looked in her green eyes and said yes. She leaned over and kissed me right on the corner of my mouth. I was so flushed, I thought I was going to pass out.

"Why did you do that?" I asked. She only smiled. I was happy she did.

The guys were looking and smiling. It all happened so suddenly that no one noticed Regina standing behind Sammy. She asked Sammy, "Do you remember me from Margulies Junior High School?"

He shook his head.

"Well, I want to know can we go out to a movie sometime. What I am asking is would you like to date or something maybe?"

Sammy turned around to face her, stood up, held her hand, looked into her eyes, and kissed her smack on the mouth. Regina nearly lost her balance.

We had attracted so much attention that we hadn't noticed Mrs. Grable watching us. She walked over and said, "There will be none of that here. This is a place for learning, not romance, do I make myself clear?"

"Yes, ma'am" was heard from the entire table. Regina hurried back to her table as Sammy still standing watched her walk away.

As she walked away, I saw the face of Sebrina Rae staring as if she knew exactly what was said. Girls tend to know these things, I guess.

As lunch continued, the guys and girls all enjoyed the rest of their meal in silence.

I walked Nikole to class, and on the way to the gym, I ran into Sebrina Rae. I was a bit nervous but stopped anyway. She said that she was happy for me and that she was inviting Mickey to her house. I asked her was she sure? She said, "Yes, he has been watching me almost each time in and out of class. I'm surprised he isn't peeking around the corner now." She giggled. "He is cute and he reminds me of Bart Simpson, dangerous in a good way."

"When are you going to ask him?"

"Right now," she said. I looked, and there was Mickey.

"Hi, Mickey, are you doing anything Friday night?"

"No," he said.

"Would you like to come over?"

"Sure, but I have to ask my parents if it's all right. You know we are new in town and my mom and dad would want to meet your parents. So if it's okay with you, they'll bring me and meet your parents at the same time."

Sebrina Rae was impressed and said, "I'll tell my parents tonight and let you know what time tomorrow."

Hoakey's mouth dropped and all he was able to say was bye.

At gym, Hoakey saw Glen and Gary. He told them what has happened and Glen laughed.

"What's so funny?" I asked.

"Mickey said to us earlier that if you didn't ask Sebrina Rae out that he would. I think you are a little jealous."

Hoakey said, "No, I don't want her to be with the wrong person. Maybe, just maybe, she feels the same for you."

Glen switched the conversation to football. He said that Jake Jr. will be starting as quarterback because of his little league experience. As we began practicing, I told Glen that he was right about Sebrina Rae and I and that I am a little bit jealous. Glen smiled and said there is nothing wrong with caring.

"You know that I liked her for a while but didn't have the guts to ask her out. Guess it wasn't meant."

"Guess not and don't be so down on yourself. You know your girl is really pretty and all the guys in the third period shop were talking about her."

"She is pretty, isn't she?"

"Coach Ward said are you two just going to talk or play ball? He said we should stay focused because the season is near and this is only our first practice. So let's get moving."

"Yes, sir," we say. We returned to the huddle and practiced like champs.

Nothing more was said, and we horsed around, showered, got dress, and went to our last class of the day.

Ms. Figuel is the history teacher. I saw a picture of her on the wall near the administrative office. She was voted the teacher of the year last year and

two years before that in our county. She was as pretty as Olivia Benson of NYPD on television.

In class, she told us that we would study the history of the world for the first couple of weeks and a test would be given at the end of the third week. There was also a field trip scheduled each month to someplace historical in the state. We all clapped in excitement. Now, let's everyone introduce themselves. In my mind, I think not again.

About five minutes after I gave my little introduction, I heard a voice that made my day; it was Nikole. I turned and there she sat two rows over and three seats back. Nikole makes me feel goofy inside. I guess that's why the guys in the movies act tough around women. This love thing can easily move you and it's only my first day.

Ms. Figuel thanked us for being cooperative and willing. She was a nice-looking woman, and when she turned sideways, she looked like Madonna.

Anyway, the bell rang, and I stopped by my locker to get my assignments and books before going to the bus.

I ran into Mickey and he was happy that he and Sebrina Rae worked things out. I told him that she is like a sister to me and that I care deeply about her. He said he understood.

I got on ahead of him and the first thing I heard was "Hoakey, come sit next to me." A little embarrassed, I lowered my head and slid in next to Nikole. She grabbed my arm, holding it as if she was hugging me.

As the bus pulled away from the school, I thank the Lord for such a marvelous day.

I looked over to Nikole as she still clung to my arm and she allowed me to kiss her on the lips. I was floored and could barely contain myself.

"What was that for?" she asked.

"No reason, I hope that I wasn't too forward."

She blushed, then lowered her head onto my shoulder.

The rest of the ride home was silent and the only thing I could hear was the beating of my heart from all the excitement.

As the bus neared the stop for us, you could hear the guys gathering their things in preparation to get off. All I could think was that the Lord is a funny guy and that He gives to those who are obedient and faithful when you least expect.

As we exit the bus, the driver says it was nice driving a quiet bus for a change. Little does he know that tomorrow is another day. Reaching the last step, I realized that I still carried the note from Nikole in my pocket and it made me smile.

Nikole asked was there something I wanted to share.

"I just realized that I still had your note in my pocket."

"Are you going to keep it?"

"Yep, I certainly am."

Glancing around, she saw her mother waiting in the car.

"Come with me so that you can meet my mother."

Nervous, I just trudged along.

Once there, I was introduced and found that her name Marseille was the same as my mother's. She said tell your parents that she and her husband would like to stop in to meet and to let you know when it's good for them.

Nikole was already in the car and was waving goodbye as I waved back.

Turning, I saw the guys standing, watching, and waiting to give me the business. I prepared for it; however, it didn't come to that. They were impressed that I had the courage to go over and meet the mother. As I did, I really did it.

Upon getting home, my mother met me at the front door with good news. She said, "Your father says no chores for you today and dinner is almost ready."

I told you God was funny. He knew how my day went and didn't want to spoil it for me. Thank you, Jesus.

I told my mother about what Nikole's mother asked and she said she'd get with dad to make sure he will be home. I also told her that they both have the same first name. She smiled and said that she must be a nice person.

As I prepared for dinner, all I could do was think about my day and Nikole. Wooooooooooooh! Then I prayed.

Lord, thank you for this day. Thank you for the food, clothing, and shelter. I know that I ask for your blessings each day, and with patience, all things come in due time. You blessed me with great first day, good teachers, new friends, and a girlfriend. I thank you for all that you have given me this day. Father, for this day, you and you alone are my forever in my heart. And I know that you didn't have to make this day as special as it was and I thank you.

Thank you and Amen.

About the Author

Wardell Henderson is from Miami, Florida, and is a retired US Air Force service member. A graduate from American Inter-Continental University in 2007 with a BA in Criminal Justice.

CPSIA information can be obtained
at www.ICGtesting.com
Printed in the USA
BVHW071525020721
611060BV00009B/953